P9-DHZ-967

Larry Gets Lost in Chicago

Illustrated by John Skewes
Written by Michael Mullin and John Skewes

little bigfoot
an imprint of sasquatch books
seattle, wa

The authors wish to thank Randy Adamsick and the Phillips family for their invaluable assistance.

Manufactured in China by C&C Offset Printing Co. Ltd. Shenzhen, Guangdong Province, in August 2015
Published by Little Bigfoot, an imprint of Sasquatch Books

20 19 18 17 16 15   15 14 13 12 11 10 9 8 7

Book design: Mint Design
Book composition: Sarah Plein

Images on page 25 were provided courtesy of The Art Institute of Chicago:

Paul Cézanne, French, 1839–1906, *The Basket of Apples*, c.1893, Oil on canvas, 25 $^7/_{16}$ x 31 ½ in. (65 x 80 cm), Helen Birch Bartlett Memorial Collection, 1926.252, The Art Institute of Chicago.

Gustave Caillebotte, French, 1848–1894, *Paris Street; Rainy Day*, 1877, Oil on canvas, 83 ½ x 108 ¾ in. (212.2 x 276.2 cm), Charles H. and Mary F. S. Worcester Collection, 1964.336, The Art Institute of Chicago.

Vincent van Gogh, Dutch, 1853–1890, *The Bedroom*, 1889, Oil on canvas, 29 x 36 ⅝ in. (73.6 x 92.3 cm), Helen Birch Bartlett Memorial Collection, 1926.417, The Art Institute of Chicago.

Library of Congress Cataloging-in-Publication Data is available

ISBN-13: 978-1-57061-619-8
ISBN-10: 1-57061-619-1

Larry adopts a food bank in every city he visits. A portion of the proceeds from this book will be donated to the Greater Chicago Food Depository. Visit its web site at www.chicagosfoodbank.org.

www.larrygetslost.com

SASQUATCH BOOKS
1904 Third Avenue, Suite 710
Seattle, WA 98101
(206) 467-4300

www.sasquatchbooks.com
custserv@sasquatchbooks.com

This is **Larry.**   This is **Pete.**

They rode on a train, each one in his seat.

Filled with excitement, they both wore a grin.
A new city **adventure** was about to begin!

Mom and Dad led the way from the big, busy station
To a water **taxi** waiting at a river location.

CHICAGO W

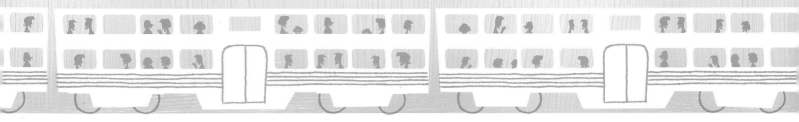

COMMUTER TRAINS

Chicago is one of the largest hubs of passenger train service in the nation. Eight rail lines bring people to Chicago's four downtown stations.

WATER TAXI

Both tourists and commuters travel the Chicago River by water taxi, from Union Station to Michigan Avenue, with stops in between at Madison and Clark Streets.

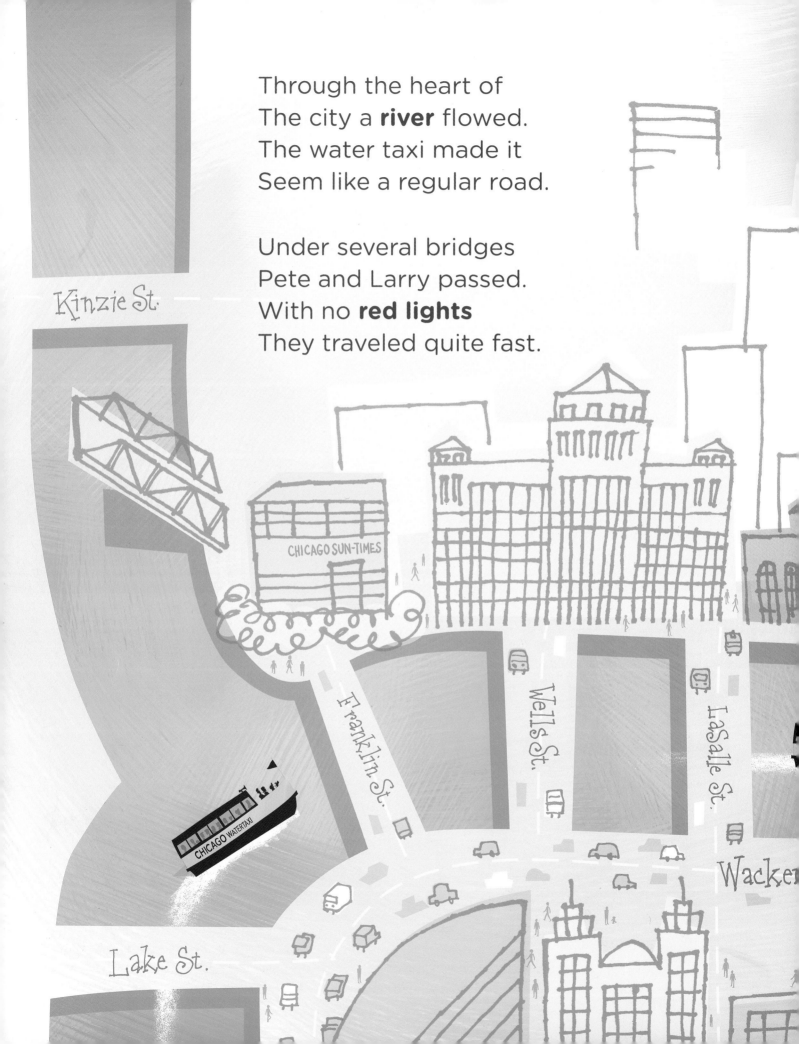

Through the heart of
The city a **river** flowed.
The water taxi made it
Seem like a regular road.

Under several bridges
Pete and Larry passed.
With no **red lights**
They traveled quite fast.

Kinzie St.

CHICAGO SUN-TIMES

Franklin St.

Wells St.

LaSalle St.

Wacker

CHICAGO WATERTAXI

Lake St.

Clark St.

Dearborn St.

STATE St.

Wabash Ave.

Michigan Ave.

Dr.

CHICAGO WATERTAXI

CHICAGO RIVER
In 1900, engineers actually reversed the direction of the Chicago River to help clean up the pollution. It used to flow into Lake Michigan. Now it flows from it.

The family walked for
What seemed like a **mile.**
So many shopping bags,
So much style.

MAGNIFICENT MILE
This part of Michigan Avenue has luxury stores and
some of the city's most famous buildings.

Larry watched a man make **hot dogs** with all kinds of stuff.
With toppings so high, would **one bun** be enough?

Mustard and **relish**
On every one,
Tomatoes, peppers,
And a seeded bun.
Celery salt (*but no **ketchup!***)
Was the **final touch.**

Larry was **SURE** Pete
Couldn't eat *that* much!

NAVY PIER

NAVY PIER
Built between 1914 and 1916, this is Chicago's most popular tourist attraction. It has a giant Ferris wheel, a carousel, and the Chicago Shakespeare Theater.

CHICAGO STYLE
HOT DOG

But eat it he did,
And Larry's **hunger** remained.
(Larry knew not to **beg.**
That was how he was trained.)

He tried to forget
His tummy frustration
As the family arrived
At a **railway** station.

Larry led them all up.
They **climbed** stair after stair.
In this part of town,
Trains are up in the air.

On the platform they waited
A minute or two
When one of those **hot dogs**
Came into view.

Larry **pounced** on it,
Happy to finally eat.
But in the time that it took . . .

THE L
"L," which is short for "elevated
train," has more than 100
miles of track connecting the
downtown Chicago Loop with
the suburbs in all directions.

. . . **He had lost
his friend Pete!**

He tried to make a
Quick **reconnection,**
But the train he jumped on
Went the *other* direction!

WRIGLEY FIELD
The home of the Chicago Cubs since 1916 is known for its ivy-covered outfield walls. It was named after William Wrigley, Jr., a former Cubs owner and founder of the Wm. Wrigley Jr. Company, famous for its chewing gum.

He was soon happy to get out,
Being packed in so **tight.**
Something big was happening
At this **round-building** site.

Could one of these people
In bright **blue** caps
Tell him where he could go
To find Pete, perhaps?

The Red Line

Addison 3600N 940W ©

Pete, Mom, and Dad rode their
Southbound train
Past a different **stadium**
With a different name.

U.S. CELLULAR FIELD
Formerly known as
Comiskey Park, this is the
home of the 2005 World
Series Champion
Chicago White Sox.

They saw trains that were big
And planes that were small,
But their search for Larry
Turned up nothing at all.

MUSEUM OF SCIENCE AND INDUSTRY
The museum features real trains, planes, jets,
a coal mine, and a German submarine!

LINCOLN PARK ZOO

The zoo opened in 1868 with only a pair of swans. Now it has more than 1,000 animals and is always free to visit.

Pete saw a statue of
A guy walking on **air.**
Larry loved to play ball,
But the pup wasn't there.

Larry stood by a lion
Who lived in a zoo,
Thinking: Thank goodness there's glass
Between me and **Big You!**

UNITED CENTER
The home of the NBA's
Chicago Bulls and the
NHL's Chicago Blackhawks.

Lake Michigan

He found a lake **shoreline**
And ran on the sand.

There were boats in the water—
And one on the **land!**

He continued his search
From way up **high . . .**

NORTH AVENUE BEACH
The Chicago Lakefront path runs 18.5 miles along the shore, connecting all of Chicago's lakefront attractions for runners, walkers, and bicyclists.

But he could not see his friend
From his place in the **sky.**

WILLIS TOWER
Formerly the Sears Tower,
this 110-story skyscraper is the
tallest building in the United
States. It has an all-glass
observation platform on the
103rd floor called "The Ledge."

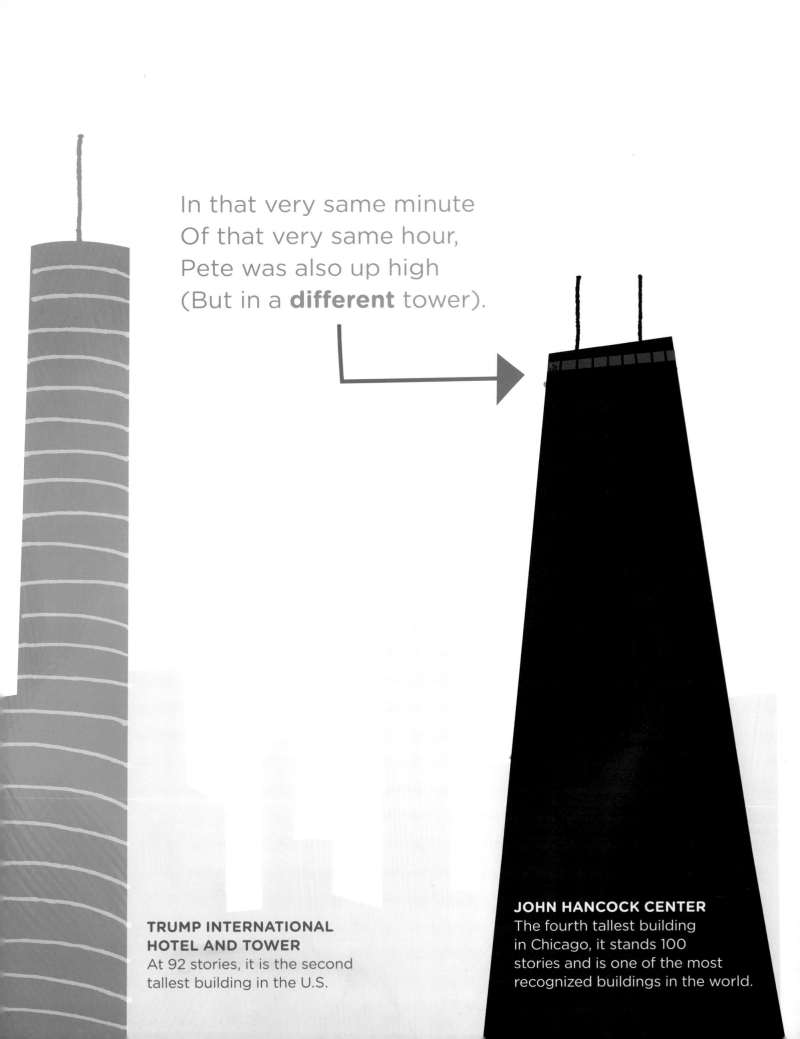

In that very same minute
Of that very same hour,
Pete was also up high
(But in a **different** tower).

**TRUMP INTERNATIONAL
HOTEL AND TOWER**
At 92 stories, it is the second
tallest building in the U.S.

JOHN HANCOCK CENTER
The fourth tallest building
in Chicago, it stands 100
stories and is one of the most
recognized buildings in the world.

No help from a **giant**
Who had nothing to say,
Nor the strange-looking lady
Who pointed **both** ways.

PUBLIC ART
Chicago is known for many public works by
famous artists, including Pablo Picasso,
Marc Chagall, Joan Miró, and Jean Dubuffet.

THE LOOP

The heart of Chicago is surrounded by a "loop" of L train tracks.

Chicago Picasso

Miró's Chicago

Meanwhile Larry met a
Monster named **Sue** . . .

. . . Saw
Beautiful
Paintings,
Old
And **new** . . .

. . . Then looked for Pete
In huge tanks of **deep blue.**

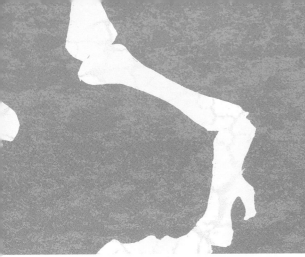

FIELD MUSEUM OF NATURAL HISTORY

Home to "Sue," the largest, most complete Tyrannosaurus rex ever discovered (but no one knows if it's a boy or a girl). The dinosaur is named after Sue Hendrickson, who discovered it.

ART INSTITUTE OF CHICAGO

The second largest museum in the U.S., the Institute has some of the world's most famous paintings.

Photography © The Art Institute of Chicago

JOHN G. SHEDD AQUARIUM

With more than 32,000 aquatic animals and 5 million gallons of water, Shedd Aquarium is one of the biggest aquariums in the world.

Millennium Park

Larry passed a round building
But stayed far away.
He heard people saying
That that's where **BEARS** play.

SOLDIER FIELD
Home of the Chicago Bears football team. Even
though Chicago is known for its cold winters, Bears
fans prefer to watch football outside.

JAY PRITZKER PAVILION
Frank Gehry designed the shiny, stainless steel
concert stage. The crisscrossing bars over the field
give it the sound of an indoor concert hall.

He ran through a park
Filled with bright, **shiny steel**
Past a crowd listening
To music in a field.

One sculpture looked like a **bean**
A giant robot might eat.
Larry saw his **reflection,**
And **beside** it . . .

CLOUD GATE
Commonly known as "the Bean," this sculpture is 66 feet long, 33 feet tall, and weighs more than 100 tons. The stainless steel surface is polished to a mirror finish.

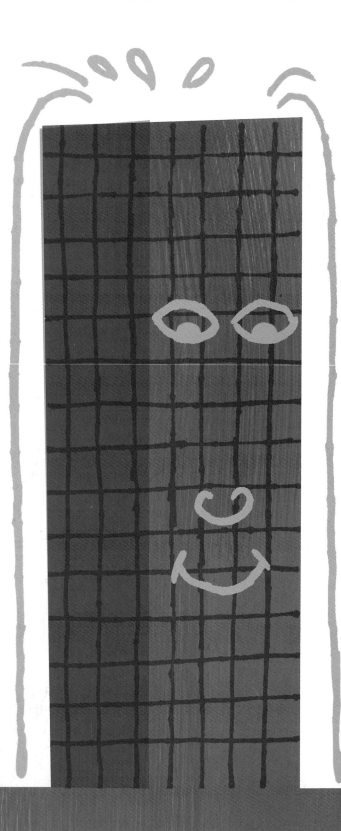

They jumped and they hugged.
He wasn't **LOST** anymore!
Then Pete saw something
They both could explore.

Two giant faces smiled at them,
Blinking their eyes.
Pete and Larry moved close
—And got a soaking **surprise!**

They passed another fountain
As they left this fun place,
But this time kept their distance
(*Just in case!*)

CROWN FOUNTAIN
These two 50-foot towers each have a giant video screen that shows one of more than 900 different faces that can "spit" real water from their mouths.

BUCKINGHAM FOUNTAIN
This fountain represents Lake Michigan, and the four horses represent the states that border the lake: Wisconsin, Illinois, Indiana, and Michigan.

They boarded a train and did their best to get dry,
And to this fabulous city, said their **"Good-bye!"**

Get More Out of This Book

On the Water

Water is a major feature of the city of Chicago. What did readers learn from the book about the Chicago River and Lake Michigan? Have readers name the different ways people travel on or over the water in Chicago. (Examples include water taxis, bridges, and commuter trains.)

A Virtual Visit

Make an online visit to the Art Institute of Chicago: www.artic.edu/aic/collections/exhibitions/Modern

- Begin by showing readers some photos of the Institute itself—the building, architecture, and interior galleries.

- Then, select some artwork to share with readers; let them spend time looking at each one while you talk about the artwork and the artist.

- Have readers choose one they like best and write or dictate a story about the artwork.

Wish You Were Here

Ask readers to choose one of the Chicago sites from the book and design a postcard for that site. Then have them write to someone "back home" about what a great time they're having in Chicago and what they're doing and seeing.

TEACHER'S GUIDE: The above discussion questions and activities are from our teacher's guide, which is aligned to the Common Core State Standards for English Language Arts for Grades K to 1. For the complete guide and a list of the exact standards it aligns with, visit our website: SasquatchBooks.com

CONGRESS HOT